This book belongs to

_____

LITTLE
RED RIDING
HOOD

LITTLE
RED RIDING HOOD

RETOLD BY
ARMAND EISEN
ILLUSTRATED BY
LYNN BYWATERS FERRIS

ARIEL BOOKS/ALFRED A. KNOPF NEW YORK 1988

THIS IS A BORZOI BOOK
PUBLISHED BY ALFRED A. KNOPF, INC.

Library of Congress Cataloging-in-Publication Data

Eisen, Armand.
Little Red Riding Hood.

(Ariel books)
Summary: A little girl meets a hungry wolf in the forest while on her
way to visit her grandmother.
[1. Fairy tales.   2. Folklore—Germany]
I. Ferris, Lynn Bywaters, ill.   II. Rotkäppchen.   III. Title.
PZ8.E36Li   1988   398.2'1 [E]   87-46241
ISBN 0-394-55883-9

Manufactured in Singapore
First Edition

The artwork in this book is dedicated
to my sister Lois.

L.B.F.

Once upon a time there was a little girl who lived with her mother in a cottage near the great woods. Everyone called the girl Little Red Riding Hood because she wore a beautiful red cloak that her grandmother had made for her.

One morning her mother said, "Little Red Riding Hood, your grandmother is ill and too weak to make her own supper. So you must take this basket of food to her. Leave now, while it is still early. But do not wander off the path or talk to any strangers along the way."

"I will do just as you say, Mother," answered Little Red Riding Hood, and off she went.

Before she had gone far into the woods, she met a large wolf.

"Good day to you, Little Red Riding Hood," he said.

"Good day to you, Wolf."

"And where are you going so early?" asked the wolf.

"To my grandmother's house."

"What is that you have in your basket?"

"It is food I am bringing to my grandmother. She is ill, and too weak to make her own supper."

"And where does your grandmother live, Little Red Riding Hood?"

"Her house is at the end of this path, in the middle of the woods."

The wolf looked at Little Red Riding Hood and thought to himself, "If I am clever, this girl and her grandmother will make a good supper for me!"

Then he said, "Do you see all the pretty flowers here in the forest? Surely your grandmother would like to have some."

"Oh yes, Grandmother loves flowers," said Little Red Riding Hood, as she stepped off the path and began picking them.

The wolf hurried away as fast as he could go.

When he reached the grandmother's house, he knocked on the door.

"Who's there?" asked the grandmother.

"It is Little Red Riding Hood," answered the wolf.

"Please come in, dear," she said.

The wolf opened the door, took one great leap forward, and swallowed the grandmother in a single gulp.

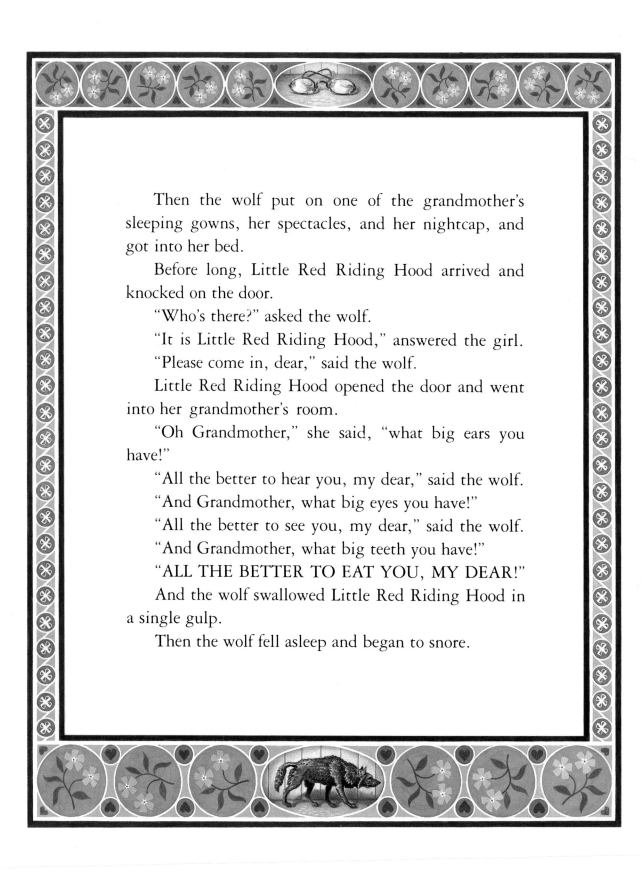

Then the wolf put on one of the grandmother's sleeping gowns, her spectacles, and her nightcap, and got into her bed.

Before long, Little Red Riding Hood arrived and knocked on the door.

"Who's there?" asked the wolf.

"It is Little Red Riding Hood," answered the girl.

"Please come in, dear," said the wolf.

Little Red Riding Hood opened the door and went into her grandmother's room.

"Oh Grandmother," she said, "what big ears you have!"

"All the better to hear you, my dear," said the wolf.

"And Grandmother, what big eyes you have!"

"All the better to see you, my dear," said the wolf.

"And Grandmother, what big teeth you have!"

"ALL THE BETTER TO EAT YOU, MY DEAR!"

And the wolf swallowed Little Red Riding Hood in a single gulp.

Then the wolf fell asleep and began to snore.

A little while later, a woodsman passing by the house heard the loud snoring. When he looked in the window he saw the sleeping wolf. So he rushed in, and with one blow of his ax chopped off the wolf's head. Out sprang Little Red Riding Hood and the grand-mother, alive and well!

They thanked the woodsman for saving them and shared their supper with him. Then Little Red Riding Hood returned home and told her mother everything that had happened. And from that day on, she never strayed off the path in the woods, or spoke to strangers, or forgot to do what her mother said.

A NOTE ON THE TYPE

The text of this book was set in a digitized version of Garamond No. 3, a
modern rendering of the type first cut by Claude Garamond (c. 1480–1561).
It is believed that Garamond based his letters on the Venetian models,
although he introduced a number of important differences, and it is to him
we owe the letter which we know as "old style."

Composed by Maxwell Photographics, Inc., New York, New York

Separations, printing, and binding by Tien Wah Press, Singapore

Art direction by Armand Eisen and Thomas Durwood

Designed by Marysarah Quinn